W9-CKC-699

DOODLE
DANDIES

doodle

poems that

w
o
r
d
s

J. Patrick Lewis

Aladdin Paperbacks
New York London Toronto Sydney Singapore

dandies
take shape

images

Lisa Desimini

with design and typography by
Ann Bobco
and
Lisa Desimini

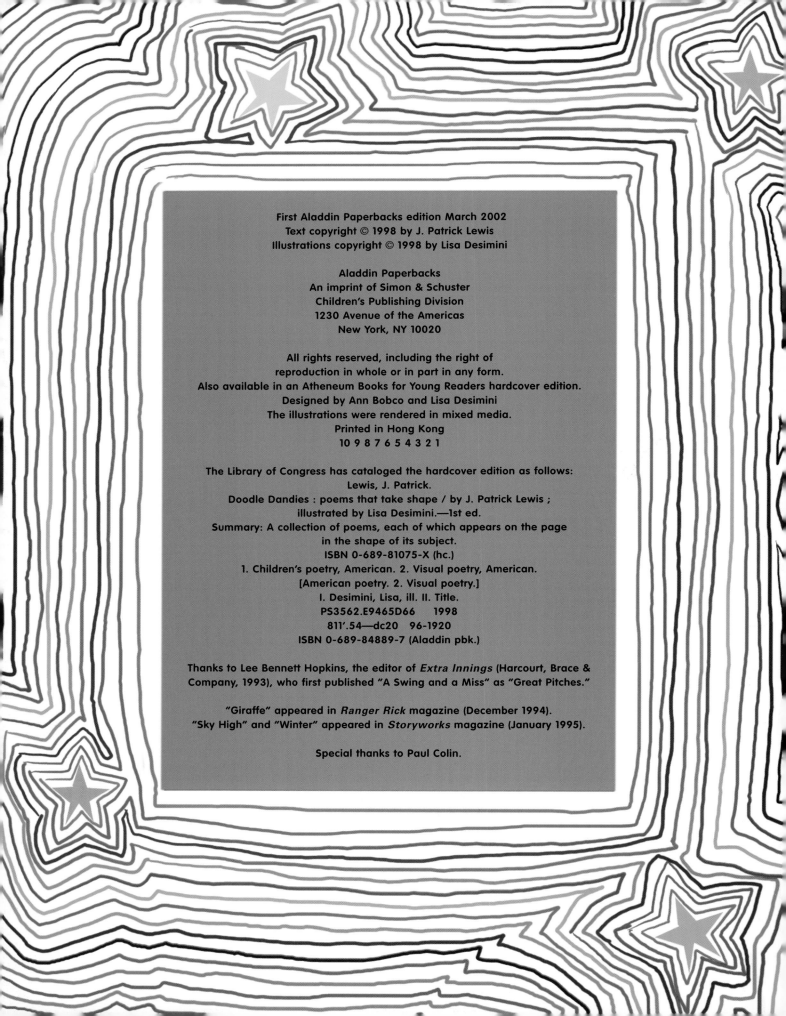

First Aladdin Paperbacks edition March 2002
Text copyright © 1998 by J. Patrick Lewis
Illustrations copyright © 1998 by Lisa Desimini

Aladdin Paperbacks
An imprint of Simon & Schuster
Children's Publishing Division
1230 Avenue of the Americas
New York, NY 10020

All rights reserved, including the right of
reproduction in whole or in part in any form.

Also available in an Atheneum Books for Young Readers hardcover edition.
Designed by Ann Bobco and Lisa Desimini
The illustrations were rendered in mixed media.
Printed in Hong Kong
10 9 8 7 6 5 4 3 2 1

The Library of Congress has cataloged the hardcover edition as follows:
Lewis, J. Patrick.
Doodle Dandies : poems that take shape / by J. Patrick Lewis ;
illustrated by Lisa Desimini.—1st ed.
Summary: A collection of poems, each of which appears on the page
in the shape of its subject.
ISBN 0-689-81075-X (hc.)
1. Children's poetry, American. 2. Visual poetry, American.
[American poetry. 2. Visual poetry.]
I. Desimini, Lisa, ill. II. Title.
PS3562.E9465D66   1998
811'.54—dc20   96-1920
ISBN 0-689-84889-7 (Aladdin pbk.)

Thanks to Lee Bennett Hopkins, the editor of *Extra Innings* (Harcourt, Brace &
Company, 1993), who first published "A Swing and a Miss" as "Great Pitches."

"Giraffe" appeared in *Ranger Rick* magazine (December 1994).
"Sky High" and "Winter" appeared in *Storyworks* magazine (January 1995).

Special thanks to Paul Colin.

JUDE

—J. P. L.

FIONA

—L. D.

First Burst
of Spring

The day is cold, the earth is mud, but

don't let anything stop you, Bud!

Dachshund

Here comes the lady with the diamond ring
walking a dog like a sausage on a string
there goes the dog with his nose in the air!
walk ing the lady with the purple hair

giraffe

Tree-tall giraffe up to his neck in brown and yellow patchwork quilts, turns tail and hobbles away on wooden stilts stilts stilts stilts

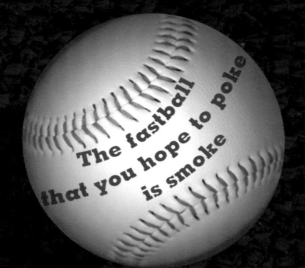

The fastball
that you hope to poke
is smoke

The screwball
an ironic twist
hits your fist

A Swing and a Miss

The knuckler
wobbling up to you
can dipsy-do

The let-up pitch
you can't resist?
you missed

The curveball
that you thought was there
is air

The sinker
comes as some surprise:
it dies

The spitball
that by law's forbidden
(is hidden)

weeping willow

Her wind-woven hair softly sweeping

In
a far
field
of
sad
ness
stands
the
wee
wid
ow
wee
ping

Skinny BONNIE Bumber wears a long, tall hat. I hide her in the closet till the clouds get fat. I poke her up and out when the sun goes away. Fattie Bonnie Bumber loves a rainy day!

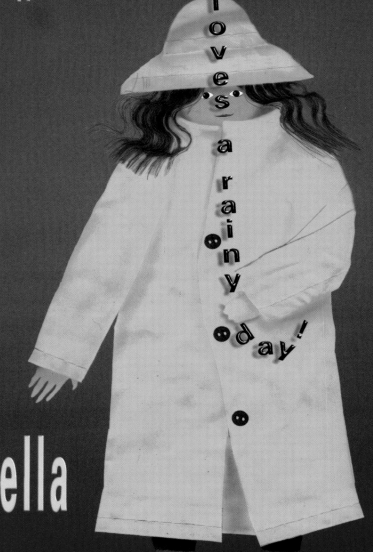

umbrella

The butterfly is

the fantasy fulfiller of every caterpillar

day delights
in jungle cries

BIG
CAT

night ignites
its tiger eyes

synchronized swim team

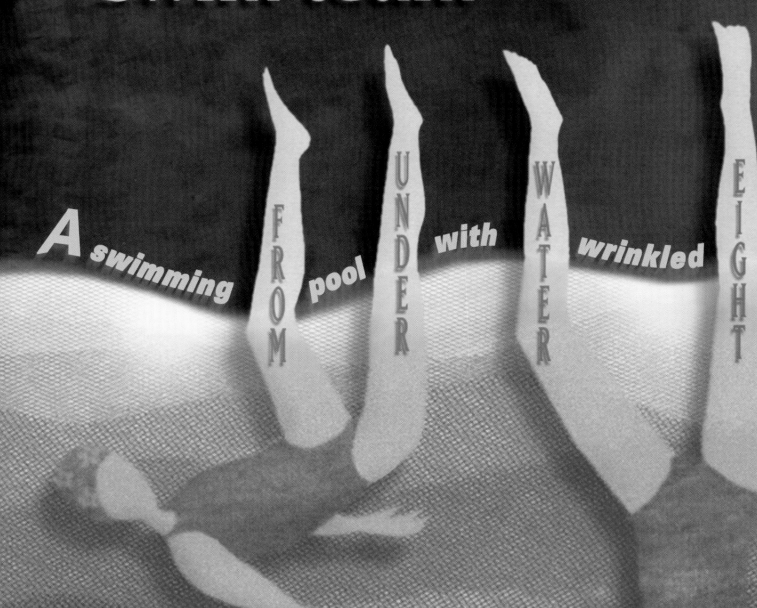

A swimming FROM pool UNDER with WATER wrinkled EIGHT

waves is **PRECISION** **NEEDLES** like a **POKING** quilt of **THROUGH** blue

The Oyster Family

An
oyster boy,
an oyster girl,
an oyster dad,
a mother-of-pearl

I slithered down to Pepper Pond for a midnight snack, a picker-upper. I missed a mouse and beetle bug, so I ate a

BULL FROG

for my supper. Well, he was tough as toad, and chewy. Mighty leggy, mighty lumpy. And let me tell you, Creep, I'm feeling mighty jumpy!

Creep and Slither

winter

when sky unravels its cold mist-eries

fluttering down brown skeletons of trees

these speckles on a page can barely show

the spectacle of unexpected snow

All eyes look down
the
cinder
track—
the
pole
vault
pole
connects,
bends
back . . .
the
boy
who's
hurled
above
the
bar
returns
to
earth
a falling
star.

Sky High

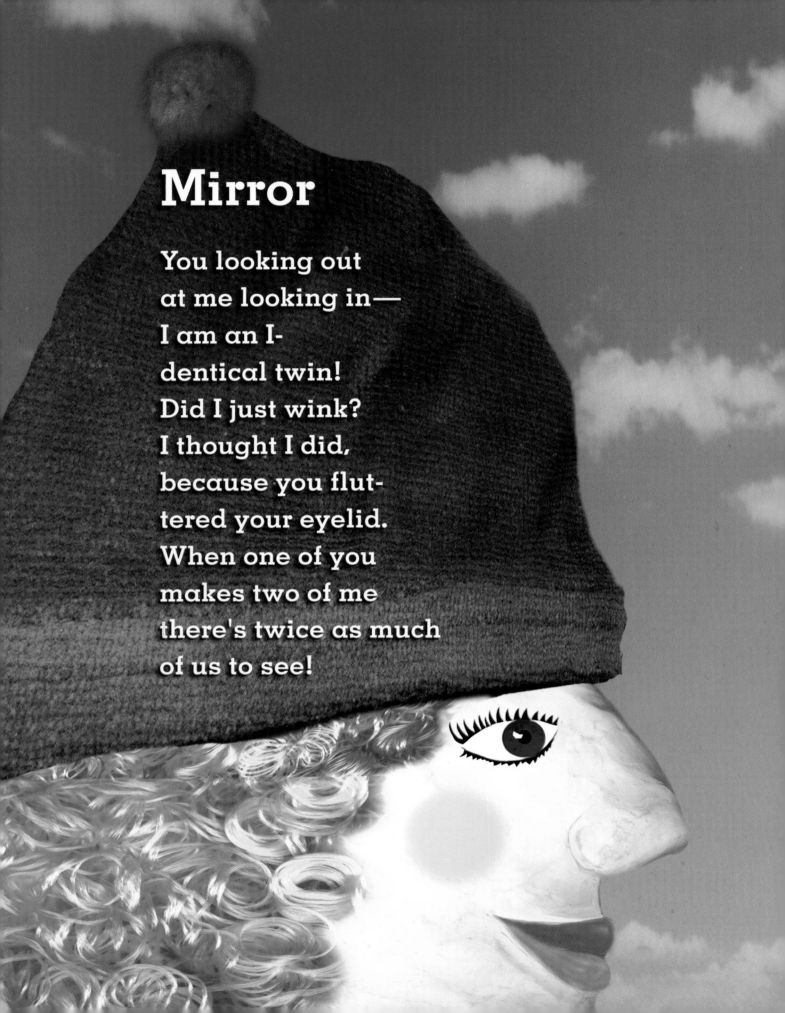

Mirror

You looking out
at me looking in—
I am an I-
dentical twin!
Did I just wink?
I thought I did,
because you flut-
tered your eyelid.
When one of you
makes two of me
there's twice as much
of us to see!

Mirror

You looking out
at me looking in—
I am an I-
dentical twin!
Did I just wink?
I thought I did,
because you flut-
tered your eyelid.
When one of you
makes two of me
there's twice as much
of us to see!

How many humps?

As the number of humps
on a camel goes,
the dromedary is

ordinary

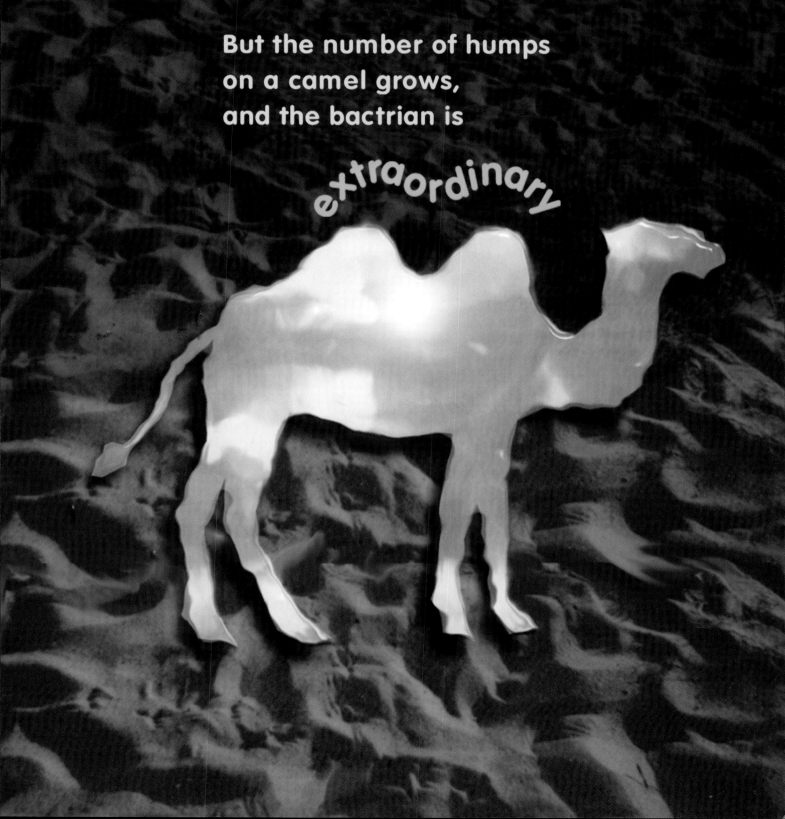

But the number of humps
on a camel grows,
and the bactrian is

extraordinary

coming ff a

Lashndra's

clck!

n the

secnds left

nly

blck!

She takes a cr●ss-

c●urt pass

from y●u and

banks it off the glass f●r

tw●

LASHONDRA
SCORES!

SKYSCRAPER

I
am
a
nee
dle
of
steel
glass &
cement
1 0 2
s t o r i e s
high on a clear
day you can see
2 0 0
miles out into the
Atlantic or watch
hundreds of ants
scurrying like
people on the sidewalks
below & the yellow
bugs racing recklessly
along the city streets &
ride the elevator all the
way down in 37 seconds
FLAT

The Turtle

is a giant hurdle

I AM
A COSMIC
SNOWBALL MADE
OF DUSTY ICE AND GAS.
ONCE OR TWICE A CENTURY
I PASS THE EARTH AND
SUN. SEE YA NEXT
TIME AROUND . . .
IN 2061!

HALLEY'S COMET